# TY
# THE T-REX



JANNELL ECTOR

# DEDICATION

Dedicated to my Treasure, whose life was cut short by gun violence. Your presence remains with me in every journey, today and always.

I'm Ty-the T-Rex, and
I love to adventure

This is my GREAT, BIG grandma – Grannysaurus. We explore together.

She is the best grandma dinosaur in the whole wide world!

I love my
Grannysaurus, and
she loves me.

We have a special
dinosaur love
between us.
We are a super
'DINO' team!

My best friend is Treasure – the T-Rex. He likes to adventure, too.

Every day, Treasure
and I explore the
world around us.

We go near and far.
We go high and low.

We stomp up
and down.
We romp left
and right.

We run fast and slow
across the forest floor.
We soar and we ROAR!

Grannysaurus is
always near –
never far!
The three of us
always have the best
T-Rex day – EVER!

Today, is an extra
special day.
We are going into the
deep forest to play.

Grannysaurus leads
the way. Wow!
There is so much to
see. I see a huge
muddy swamp.


Splash!
I jump in like a
mighty T-Rex king.

Oh, no!
This mud is too heavy
for me to swim.

My arms are too tiny
and short to reach
for Treasure's hand. I
am stuck!

But my GREAT, BIG
Grannysaurus
knows what to do.
She uses her huge
teeth to pull
me out.

I kind of look silly
covered head to
tail in mud
but – HOORAY!
Grannysaurus saves
the day.

We run fast and slow across the forest floor. We soar and we ROAR!

She takes us to a
clean water hole.
And grandma is the
first to jump in.
SPLASH!

Treasure jumps in
after her.
SPLASH! He looks
so happy.

clap

Whee! I slide my way into the water for all the more fun!

The mud is off. I am so happy to be clean again. Treasure has a fun idea about how we can get dry, fast.

We stretch east
and west.
We reach north
and south.
We bend this and
that way in the
cool wind.


Ripppppp! Uh oh!
I tear my pants as
I try to reach way
past Treasure
this time.

Grannysaurus says
she can fix it
at home.
Treasure thinks we
can tippy toe all
the way.
Shhhhhhh!

We have so much
fun trying –
But being quiet is not
that easy for any
T-Rex, dinosaur KING!

Back home,
Grannysaurus fixes
my pants.
But I chase
Treasure around
and it rips again.

She gives me a new
pair of pants, and
a GREAT, BIG,
dinosaur hug.
I am so happy she
NEVER gets mad.

My Grannysaurus is truly the best grandma that any T-Rex could ever hope to have.

I wonder where we will adventure tomorrow.
I bet anywhere will be just perfect with just Grannysaurus, Treasure and me!

# THE END